GRUMPY LOST AND FOUND IN NAPLES

(A Grumpy the Iguana and Green Parrot Adventure)

By: Susan Marie Chapman

Illustrated by: Natalia Loseva

For Mitch and Elle

Published 2023

Printed in the United States of America
Print ISBN: 978-1-7368056-7-1

Canoe Tree Press
4697 Main Street
Manchester, VT 05255
www.CanoeTreePress.com

Grumpy the Iguana climbed down from his tree home and stretched his legs. "Oh, what a glorious day," Grumpy thought to himself.

It was a chilly morning in Flamingo Park.
Winters in Florida can get very cold,
especially when temperatures drop
below 40 degrees Fahrenheit.

40 is the magic number that turns happy-go-lucky iguanas moving quickly through the park, into frozen Popsicles, instantly.

When it's cold, the iguanas' little hands and feet freeze up so that they lose all control of their body parts and just fall from the tree branches. "Oh no," they seem to say as they fall to the ground.

But don't worry; as soon as the temperature rises, they will thaw out and be able to move around again, unharmed.

Iguanas are cold-blooded and cannot endure extreme temperature drops. Iguanas rely on natural sunlight and tropical climate conditions to survive. This process is called homeostasis.

Living somewhere warm is the most important of these conditions. That is why we can only find iguanas in the states of Texas, Florida, and Hawaii.

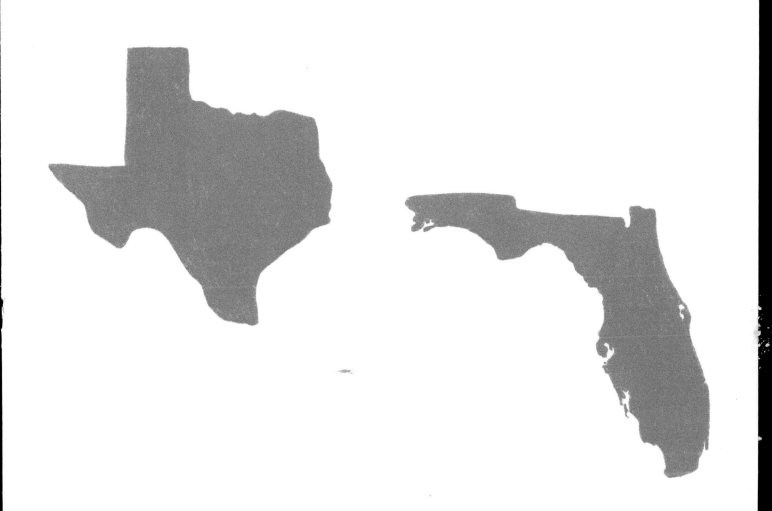

Grumpy shuddered at the thought of being cold as he meandered through the park. He paused briefly to watch a human family spread a huge blanket out on the grass.

He was curious. That blanket looked warm and cozy. Grumpy made a split-second decision and quickly crawled underneath the blanket and fell fast asleep.

It was late afternoon when the family packed up their belongings to head home.

Grumpy could not escape as he was
scooped up, along with the large blanket,
and placed into the trunk of the car.

He lay there very still in the darkness of the
trunk waiting for a chance to get away.
Grumpy had no idea what had
happened or where he was.

He thought about his tree home and his friends. Although he was trying to be brave, Grumpy started to cry. He wondered if his roommate, the Green Parrot, noticed that he was missing.

Maybe help was on the way.

Finally the car stopped and someone lifted the blanket out of the trunk. Grumpy tried to hang on but instead fell onto the curb unnoticed. He quickly crawled under a large bush.

He stayed hidden until it was quiet and he felt safe. Grumpy slowly stuck his head out and looked around. His eyes widened. "Where am I?" Grumpy whispered to himself. Nothing looked familiar.

He started to crawl toward the nearest tree when he realized that he was in a park, but what park? He looked for his friends, Green Parrot and Mr. Squirrel, but could not hear or see them anywhere.

Grumpy stood very still. He could hardly breathe and his heart began beating faster and faster, as he realized that he was no longer in Flamingo Park.

"Are you an iguana?" said a tiny voice.
Grumpy looked down at his feet and noticed
a little red ladybug looking up at him.

"Why, yes, I am," Grumpy answered. "Can you tell me what park this is, Miss Ladybug?"

"Hehehe!" she laughed.
"Do you mean to tell me that you don't know
where you are?" Miss Ladybug shouted.
Grumpy looked around and then at Miss Ladybug.
"Yes," he answered nervously.

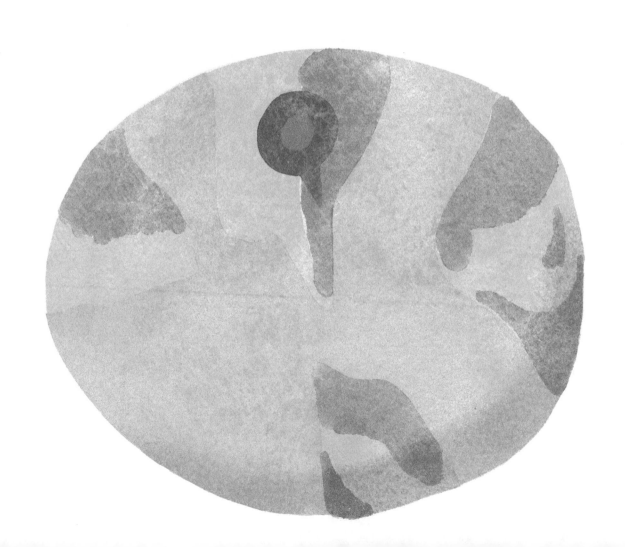

"You are in Cambier Park, my dear iguana. Welcome to Naples, Florida," the little ladybug explained.

"Naples?" Grumpy replied, shocked. He had never heard of Naples before. "Miss Ladybug, do you know where Flamingo Park is?" Grumpy asked.

"Nope, never heard of that park," snapped the little ladybug, as she scurried away.

Grumpy put his head in his hands and started to cry. "How am I ever going to find my way home?" he thought to himself.

He then walked through the entire park, looking up into every tree for anything familiar until he came upon a rather large sign that said, "Welcome To Cambier Park."

He slowly crossed the street and was now sitting on the steps of the Naples Fire and Rescue Station. He was scared and lost and had no idea what to do next.

All of a sudden, a voice shouted, "Grumpy, thank goodness, I found you!" Grumpy looked up. He would know that voice anywhere.

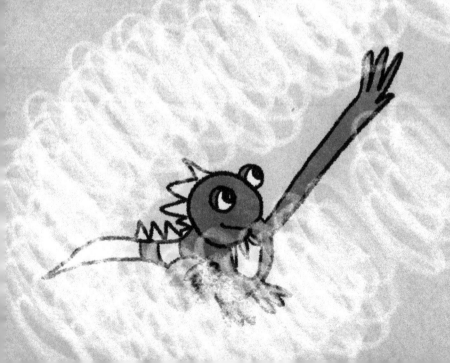

The Green Parrot was standing in front of him with his hands on his hips.

"Green Parrot, are you lost too? You don't know how happy I am to see you," Grumpy shouted as he jumped up and gave his best friend and roommate a big hug.

"I am not lost," the Green Parrot replied.
"I followed you here from Miami Beach
after I witnessed the human family
drive off with you in their car."

"I am so grateful and happy that you found me. Now let's go home." Grumpy sighed.

"I am afraid that's impossible. We are now on the West Coast of Florida," the Green Parrot explained. "Flamingo Park is all the way on the East Coast of Florida, which is about two hours away as the crow (or parrot) flies. It would probably take you a whole year to walk that far, Grumpy."

W

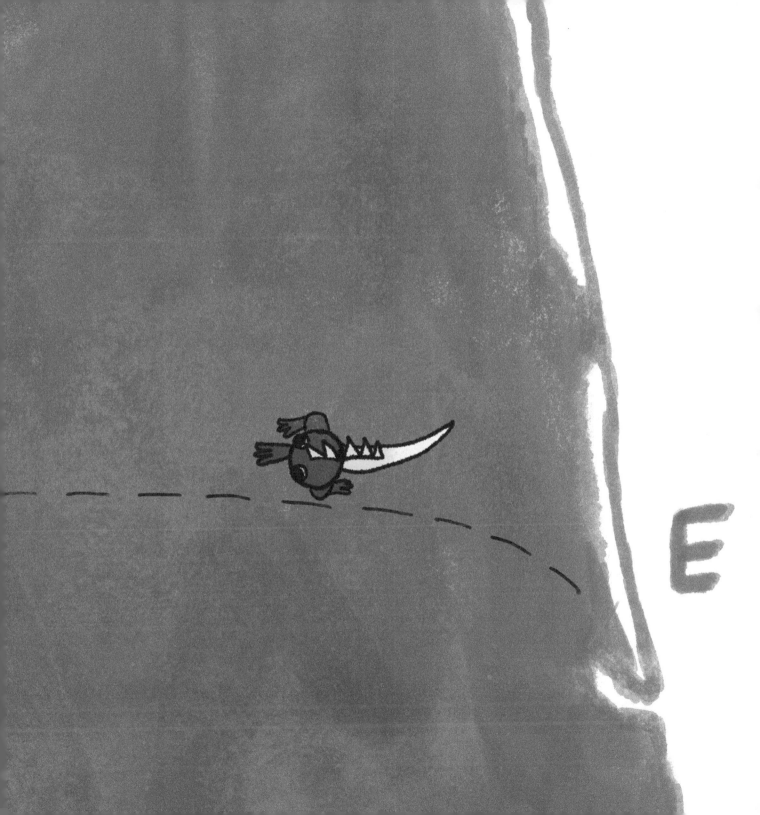

E

"Well, what do we do now?" Grumpy asked, looking to his friend for a solution.

"I am afraid there's no going back," the Green Parrot sadly replied. "Naples is now our new home, and we are going to make the best of it."

"Just think of the possibilities,"
the Green Parrot said, smiling.

The End

Continue the adventure with the next story
in the Grumpy the Iguana and Green Parrot series.

CPSIA information can be obtained
at www.ICGtesting.com
Printed in the USA
BVHW061011270423
663155BV00006B/297